Dear Parent:

Congratulations! Your child is taking the first steps on an exciting journey. The destination? Independent reading!

STEP INTO READING® will help your child get there. The program offers books at five levels that accompany children from their first attempts at reading to reading success. Each step includes fun stories, fiction and nonfiction, and colorful art. There are also Step into Reading Sticker Books, Step into Reading Math Readers, and Step into Reading Phonics Readers— a complete literacy program with something to interest every child.

Learning to Read, Step by Step!

Ready to Read Preschool–Kindergarten
• big type and easy words • rhyme and rhythm • picture clues
For children who know the alphabet and are eager to begin reading.

Reading with Help Preschool–Grade 1
• basic vocabulary • short sentences • simple stories
For children who recognize familiar words and sound out new words with help.

Reading on Your Own Grades 1–3
• engaging characters • easy-to-follow plots • popular topics
For children who are ready to read on their own.

Reading Paragraphs Grades 2–3
• challenging vocabulary • short paragraphs • exciting stories
For newly independent readers who read simple sentences with confidence.

Ready for Chapters Grades 2–4
• chapters • longer paragraphs • full-color art
For children who want to take the plunge into chapter books but still like colorful pictures.

STEP INTO READING® is designed to give every child a successful reading experience. The grade levels are only guides. Children can progress through the steps at their own speed, developing confidence in their reading, no matter what their grade.

Remember, a lifetime love of reading starts with a single step!

www.stepintoreading.com

Educators and librarians, for a variety of teaching tools, visit us at
www.randomhouse.com/teachers

Library of Congress Cataloging-in-Publication Data
Berenstain, Stan, 1923– .
The Berenstain Bears catch the bus : a tell the time story / The Berenstains.
   p.   cm. — (Step into reading. A step 2 book)
SUMMARY: As the minutes pass and the school bus gets closer to their house, Brother
and Sister are in increasing danger of missing it.
ISBN 0-679-89227-3 (trade) — ISBN 0-679-99227-8 (lib. bdg.)
[1. Bears—Fiction. 2. Time—Fiction. 3. Punctuality—Fiction. 4. Stories in rhyme.]
I. Berenstain, Jan, 1923– . II. Title. III. Series: Step into reading. Step 2 book.
PZ8.3.B4493 Bgv 2003 [E]—dc21 2002015699

Printed in the United States of America 32 31 30 29

The Berenstain Bears

CATCH THE BUS

A TELL THE TIME STORY

The Berenstains

Random House 🏠 New York

6:59

It is almost seven,
as you can see.
All is quiet
in the Bears'
Home Sweet Tree.

The cubs are asleep
at seven o'clock.
The alarm goes off.
It is quite a shock.

7:05

Five minutes later,
they are back to sleep.
Brother and Sister
are back to sleep!

Papa's coffee
starts to perk.
Papa will soon
be going to work.

And off to work
goes Grizzly Gus,
the driver of
the cubs' school bus.

7:20

The school bus starts

on its way

to pick up cubs

for school today.

7:25

What about Brother
and Sister Bear?
Will they be ready
when Gus gets there?

The bus stops here.

The bus stops there.

It picks up bear

after bear after bear.

Will our cubs be ready?

It is a worry.

They may not be—

unless they hurry.

19

7:35

But are <u>they</u> worrying?

They are not.

Are they hurrying?

They are not.

7:40

Gus picks up Bob
and Liz and Fred.
<u>Are</u> Brother and Sister
<u>still in bed?</u>

7:45

Ma sees the bus.

She starts to worry.

To catch that bus,

her cubs must hurry.

But upstairs there is not
a single sound—
the cubs are not even
up and around!

No more dreams
for Sister and Brother.
They wake up to
an angry mother.

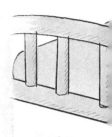

The old school bus is
almost there—
at the house of
Brother and Sister Bear!

7:50

7:55

7:56

Hurry! Hurry!

Rush! Rush! Rush!

7:57

Wash and dress.

Comb and brush.

7:58

Downstairs! Downstairs
in a flash!

7:59

Eat some breakfast!
Off you dash!

8:00

At eight o'clock,
they catch the bus
and say hello
to Grizzly Gus!

Moral:

If you sleep past seven,

you might be late

when the school bus comes

for you at eight!